# Toby and His Old Tin Tub

written and illustrated by
Colin West

PICTURE WINDOW BOOKS
Minneapolis, Minnesota

Managing Editor: Catherine Neitge
Story Consultant: Terry Flaherty
Page Production: Melissa Kes
Creative Director: Keith Griffin
Editorial Director: Carol Jones

First American edition published in 2006 by
Picture Window Books
5115 Excelsior Boulevard
Suite 232
Minneapolis, MN 55416
1-877-845-8392
www.picturewindowbooks.com

First published in Great Britain by
A & C Black Publishers Limited
37 Soho Square, London W1D 3QZ
Text and illustrations copyright © 2005 Colin West

Library of Congress Cataloging-in-Publication Data
West, Colin.
Toby and his old tin tub / written and illustrated by Colin West.
p. cm. — (Read-it! chapter books)
Summary: While sailing in his tin bathtub, Toby encounters a lonely giant who is
seeking the sound that will awaken the inhabitants of the island he guards.
ISBN 1-4048-1279-2 (hard cover)
[1. Bathtubs—Fiction. 2. Giants—Fiction. 3. Hiccups—Fiction. 4. Islands—Fiction.]
I. Title. II. Series.
PZ7.W51744Tob 2005
[E]—dc22                        2005007189

# Table of Contents

# Chapter One

Toby wanted to be a sailor, but he didn't know much about the sea. And all he had for a boat was an old tin bathtub.

One day, Toby was feeling very adventurous.
He paddled his tub an extra long way out from
his home in Puddledock Beach.

He spent some time drifting around ...

trying to think up a name for his trusty tub.

Soon Toby fell fast asleep.

It was about supper time when Toby finally woke up. He was disappointed he hadn't come up with a good name for his tub.

Then he looked about, and, to his horror, he realized he couldn't see the shore!

The sky was getting darker, and the sea was getting rougher. Then there was a clap of thunder and a flash of lightning.

Toby's tiny tub was tossed up and down by the huge waves.

# Chapter Two

The storm raged all night long, but somehow Toby's tub survived. Slowly, the clouds disappeared and the sea became calm again.

When Toby looked around, he saw he was in a very strange place.

There were tall icebergs towering over him, and in the distance was a big island with two smaller islands nearby.

As Toby paddled toward the small islands, he could see they weren't made of ice or rock or sand.

Toby prodded one of them with his oar.
He had the shock of his life when suddenly,
it moved!

"OUCH!" bellowed a mighty voice. And, looming above him, Toby saw the face of a massive sea giant. He realized he'd just prodded the giant's kneecap.
Toby was frightened.

But there was something about the sea giant that didn't make him look fierce and mean. He looked miserable.

Toby realized there was no need to
be scared. This was a harmless giant.
"What's the matter?" asked Toby.
"It's a long story," replied the sea
giant, whose name was Blubber.

# Chapter Three

It seemed that almost two hundred years ago,
King Krug, the king of all sea giants, had
placed Blubber in charge of the island
of Dumbfoundland.

The Echoless Icebergs

Big Hush Harbor

The Quiet Caves

The Sleeping Burrows

The Voiceless Rocks

Dumbfoundland

Now, Dumbfoundland was a special sort of place. It was home to lots of very odd creatures, but they were all fast asleep in secret caves and burrows. And it needed a magic sound to wake them up.

21

Unfortunately, no one knew what magic sound was needed. Blubber was desperate for some friends. So, for two hundred years, he'd been trying all the noises he could think of to wake up the animals.

Blubber had tried ...

singing

and howling

and screaming

and growling.

And he'd tried yelling and barking and roaring and squawking.

And also wailing and mooing and
hissing and booing.

And not forgetting ...

coughing

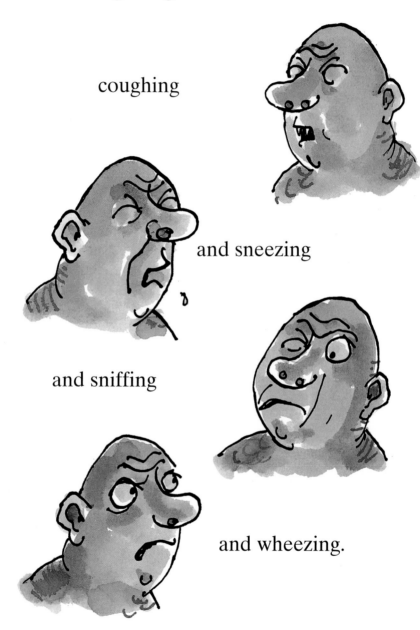

and sneezing

and sniffing

and wheezing.

But Dumbfoundland had remained as
sleepy as ever. So Blubber had tried
making up new noises.

He'd thurped and thoogled and woppled
and googled. But still it was no use.

Blubber was really lonely.

Finally, he'd sobbed and sighed and
moaned and cried from being all alone
for two hundred years.

# Chapter Four

Toby could see just how sad the sea giant felt. He thought the best thing to do was to cheer him up. So Toby told Blubber the funniest joke he knew.

At first, the sea giant began to chuckle to himself. Then his laughter grew louder, and his huge body started shaking. He wriggled his toes, and he thumped his knees.

And he laughed so much that he started
to hiccup.

They were the loudest hiccups Toby had ever heard.

And as the hiccups echoed all around,
Toby heard a flapping noise and a splashing
sound. And then it happened.

A strange bird flew overhead ...

and a funny fish
leapt out of the water.

# Chapter Five

Toby suddenly realized that the sound of hiccups was the magic sound needed to wake up all the strange animals.

So Toby told more and more jokes to Blubber as fast as he could.

What's yellow and dangerous?

Shark-infested custard!

What do scientists eat?

Microchips!

What's hairy and wears sunglasses?

A coconut on vacation!

What's green and points north?

A magnetic cucumber!

What's the fastest vegetable?

A runner bean!

What do ghosts eat for supper?

Ghoulash!

Blubber couldn't stop laughing. And the
more he laughed, the more he hiccuped.

And the more he hiccuped, the more
the strange birds flapped and the more
the funny fish splashed.

Then some really odd creatures started
appearing from the hidden caves
and the secret burrows.

41

There were all sorts, such as ...

the green
thingy,

the oink,

the willet,

the rippersaurus,

the slopp,

the great thump,

and the wasseltrope.

Blubber was the happiest sea giant
in the world, as he played with all his
newfound friends.

Toby could have stayed all day, but he knew he should be getting home. So he waved goodbye and paddled away in his old tin tub.

# Chapter Six

As the sound of hiccups faded into the distance, Toby realized he still hadn't thought up a name for his tub. So that's what he tried to do.

Suddenly, Toby had something else to think about. He noticed that a thick fog was rolling over him.

Soon Toby couldn't see a thing, but he kept on paddling.

48

After a long, long time, Toby could just
make out a dim light in the distance.

As he came closer, he could see it was
coming from a lighthouse.

He was back home at Puddledock Beach!

And as he recalled his adventure, Toby
suddenly knew what to call his old tin tub—
The Hiccup, of course!

# About the author

Colin West studied graphic design in college, and studied illustration at the Royal College of Art in London. He has written more than 50 children's books.

# Look for More
## *Read-It!*
## Chapter Books

*Bricks for Breakfast* by Julia Donaldson

*Duncan and the Pirates* by Peter Utton

*Hetty the Yeti* by Dee Shulman

*The Mean Team from Mars* by Scoular Anderson

*Spookball Champions* by Scoular Anderson

Looking for a specific title or level? A complete list
of *Read-it!* Chapter Books is available on our Web site:
**www.picturewindowbooks.com**